At the Pig Races

Written By Deborah Burggraaf

Illustrated By Matthew Lumsden

1.20.16   *Deborah Burggraaf*   dburgg.com

ISBN 978-0-9857105-9-0
Library of Congress Control Number 2012946715

Published
By
Protective Hands Communications
Riviera Beach, FL 33404
Toll free: 866-457-1203
www.protectivehands.com
steve@protectivehands.com

Printed in the United States of America

DEDICATION

To dear friends
and
the most dedicated swine lovers I know,

MARYANN and DON MILLER
of
Loxahatchee, Florida

Deborah Burggraaf

To Jaci and Jimbo, love you guys.
Matt Lumsden

It was summer and that meant only one thing for every child — school was finally out and no more homework!

As the children jumped with joy, they were also celebrating the first day of the County Fair.

Nearly everyone in this small town of Danbury would attend this annual event.

Full of excitement and tickets in hand, the children all rushed to the fair lines. Displays of ice cream cones swirled around with colorful sprinkles, as Abe Lincoln walked tall on stilts waving our great, American flag.

There were booths filled with red, candy apples, over-stuffed bags of kettle corn and pink, cotton candy. Children cried out for samples of each, as families made their way through the ticket gate to the first stop, *Yesteryear Village*.

Here, the children watched, as Railroad Engineers displayed their craft of miniature railways with steaming locomotives. There were working street lights, old windmills pumping water, and even a replica of a Ferris Wheel turning, with little people holding on tight.

As children made their way through this moment in time, they entered into *Baskets in Bloom*. Weavers from the past came to life, as they demonstrated treasured skills using long strands of straw, each a piece of wonderful art.

Eyes opened wide like colorful flowers, as stories were shared about these masterpieces.

As the families exited, off they went into the *Farmer's Showcase* and the *Petting Zoo*. Inside this vast building were cows, along with bails of hay and large trays of water. Next to them, were the cooing chickens, clacking ducks and cawing roosters. And then, there were the pigs!

Oh, the children were so excited to see the pigs: Yorkshire, Poland China, and even Japanese Pot Bellies.

"Just wait, the pig races come later," called out one father. "It's a must see event at the Fair," he added.

The children bent over to look at the roosters in all of their glory with shiny feathers adorned with golden crowns, as if they were the kings and queens of the Fair! On the stage was the *Rooster Cawing Contest*. Two boys and a young girl were mimicking the rooster's caw. One boy had the best rooster caw and won the *Rooster Caw Trophy!*

Just outside of the gate was the *Petting Zoo*. Parents held on to their children's hands as they approached the small creatures. There were sheep, and even a lamb that had been born the night before. For 25 cents, children could feed the animals. The lamb tickled the young girl's palm.

As the morning approached early noon, the families made their way to the *Food Court*, full of tasty, tempting treats for every imagination. There were deep-fried, cinnamon twists, crunchy zucchini and plump, juicy hot dogs. The selection of food was endless! People could make choices from many bountiful booths: French fries to Greek salads; chicken ka-bobs to huge, turkey legs. The children's eyes were bigger than their bellies, so parents often made their selections for them, encouraging them to finish one item at a time.

All of the families shared the large, picnic tables. Directly behind the Food Court was the *Midway*, with all of the crazy, fair rides. The children begged to go on the rides right after eating their final bites of food.

Parents suggested one more stop before going on the rides, and of course, the big event of the day, are the *PIG RACES* at 3:00 pm.

Off they went to the *Midway*, full of scary rides and even a fun, fishing game for the little ones. Parents held on tight to their children's hands, as they made their way through the growing crowds.

First, was the *Bungee Drop*, for the adventurous teens. And of course, everyone enjoys the *roller coaster*, roaring above the crowds of heads, as it makes it way around, swirling high above the Fair. At the *Haunted House*, youngsters were greeted at the door with the evil eyes of the scarecrow, inviting in the fearless, if they dared to enter!

Next, parents took the small children over to, "*Fishing Sticks*," where everyone is a winner and receives a small, stuffed toy for their catch. Children lined up with their fishing poles, trying to hook bobbing, plastic fish from the pool of water.

"Up, up...here it comes," called out one youngster, flipping his plastic fish into the air.

"We've got a WINNER!" declared the attendant behind the blue, water tank. The young boy selected a stuffed, yellow and black fish with stripes, affectionately hugging his prize catch.

Directly behind the *Midway*, was the *Ferris Wheel*. Families lined up, climbing into the deep buckets on this all-time Fair favorite.

"Hold on tight," the fair attendant advised.

As the motor started, the children held on and began to rise up, higher and higher, until they had reached the top of the Fair and could see everything below.

'What a wonderful world,' a song familiar to many, serenaded the riders, as their hearts filled with amazement.

"Now can we go and see the *Pig Races*?" asked the little girl in the pink pants.

"We must go now," reassured her father, "as we want to get good seats."

"We will go on the other rides later," her mother suggested, reaching for her hand.

At 3:00 pm, there are two *pig races*, or "*heats*," for the entire Fair to enjoy. Families began taking their seats on the sections of wooden bleachers, searching out the best view for the *Pig Races*, the main event for fairgoers every year.

"Ladies and Gentleman, and children of all ages, welcome to this year's best, *Hog-Wild Pig Races* in the country! I am your Swine Master of Ceremony today. But before we get going, I want to know, how many of you have *never* been to the Pig Races before?"

"Well, we got quite a few of you out there," he observed, as the jubilant crowd raised their hands.

"Now, we are ready to bring out our Hog Racin' Wonders of the day—Here they are!" cried the Swine Master.

The country music played in the background, as the pigs made their way around the straw-filled racetrack.

But way back in the swine tent, away from all of the big crowds and happy cheering, was Glorious Gabby, a Poland China pig. She traveled with her pig family who had raced in all of the races.

But Glorious Gabby could not race. Gabby was bowlegged and was always left behind the other pigs. She always dreamed of being a racer like the others, but her legs had never allowed her any speed.

"And now, here are our wild pigs for our first heat of the day," continued the Swine Master, as Glorious Gabby listened intently. "Our number one pig is Wild Willy." As he was introduced, Wild Willy made his way to the gate.

"Let's hear it for Wild Willy!"

"And here is our second pig in our first race, number two is Macho Mac!" The crowd clapped and clapped. "Our third pig today is Sassy Suzie," he continued, as the crowd was now standing on their feet. "And the final pig in our first heat of the day is, Dumplin' Donny," announced the Swine Master to a standing crowd.

Glorious Gabby was in the tent, listening to the names of her family being called.
Sadly, blue tears dropped from her true, ebony eyes.
   'I can do this! I know I can race like the others,' she thought.

"Now folks, at the sound of the bell, let's begin our first pig race of the day!"

Off went the bell, as the pigs slowly began to race around the straw racetrack. They made their way around the circle of waving, red, white and blue flags, as the crowd roared.

But the crowd could not hear the sadness of Glorious Gabby's heart weeping in the tent behind the races.

Glorious Gabby stood up, dried her tears, and thought one more time, 'I can do this; I *can* win!'

With that, she began running around the tent, all alone, from one end to the other. She could hear the Swine Master calling the race. "And we have Wild Willy edging up in front of Macho Mac. And behind Macho Mac is Sassy Suzie, comin' up from behind." "It's Macho Mac out in front, followed by Sassy Suzie..."

"It's Sassy Suzie leading, followed by Dumplin' Donny, trailing right behind." "It looks like Dumplin' Donny and Sassy Suzy! It's Dumplin' Donny....*he's the winner*!" confirmed the Swine Master.

"Okay, let's get our number one pig cheerer down to the microphone."

"Where are you, young man?" asked the Swine Master above the crowd of applause.

Back in the tent, Glorious Gabby could only hope for her chance to make it to the racetrack.

The little boy with the big, cowboy hat made his way down from the top of the bleachers to collect his prize. A pig nose was placed over his head and he was handed coupons for sweet, fair treats. The crowd roared with enthusiasm!

All together, the country music enchanted the crowd to clap for the final *pig race* of the day.

"And now, for our final heat of the day, folks, let's give a big welcome for our racing pigs!" cheered the Swine Master.

"Let's welcome, pig number one, 'Ole Oscar. And, let's give it up for our pig number two today, here comes Winkin' Winnie." The people continued their applause.

As the third pig made his way out to the gate, the Swine Master announced his appearance. "And here comes our number three swine. Folks, let's welcome Merry Missy!"

Just then, as the pig trainers were trying to move the number four pig out from the tent and onto the straw racetrack, something happened! Alpha Andy would not budge!

Alpha Andy sat up, and then he lay down. He sat up again, and then he rolled over onto his side. Alpha Andy would not move, even with the most enticing treat.

The swine helpers quickly removed his number 4 badge from his back. Dumbfounded, the trainers turned to each other with puzzled looks on their faces.

As the swine trainers looked across the tent, they could see Glorious Gabby running with full steam ahead. Finally, one of the trainers called her over to the race track entrance.

"Come on girl, it's your time to race; you're our lucky number 4 today!" He patted Glorious Gabby on her pink and brown spotted back.

Glorious Gabby couldn't believe her ears! She whined and whinnied and ran over to her trainers. They quickly adorned her with the number 4 badge.

"And finally, here comes our lucky number 4 swine for our final pig race of the day. Let's hear it for Gor-ge-ous, Glor-i-ous Gabby," announced the Swine Master, in his loudest voice ever.

The little girl in the pink pants stood up in the front row, and called out, "You're a winner, Gabby, you're a *WINNER*!"

Glorious Gabby heard her name called and proudly walked through the gate for the first time ever. Glorious Gabby was ready to race, knowing that, '*I am a Winner*.'

The beat of the drums filled the hearts of the audience, followed by the familiar bugle sound that Glorious Gabby had only listened to before from the tent. Finally, the gate opened for her for the first time in her life.

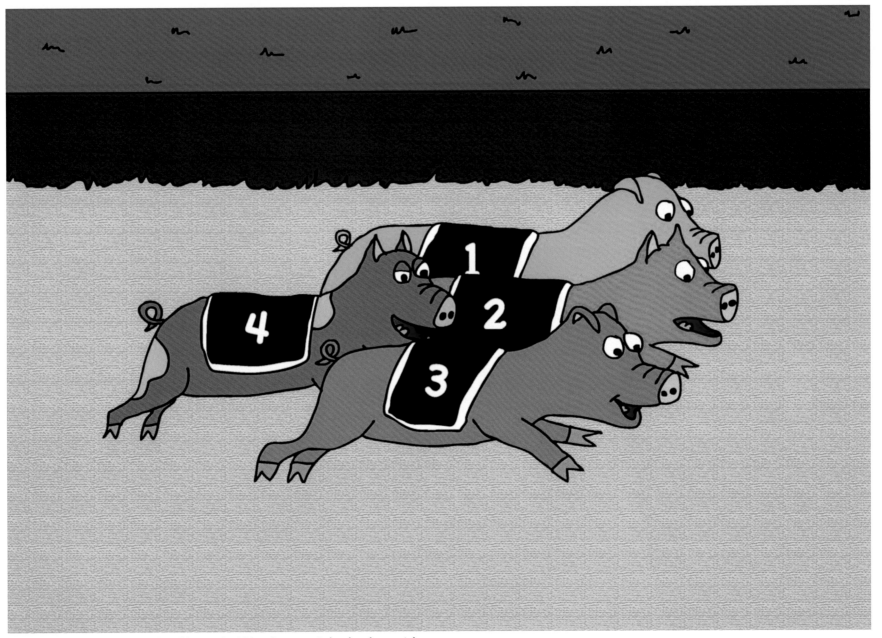

Glorious Gabby took off, with 'Ole Oscar right by her side.

"And it's Winkin' Winnie taking the lead, followed by 'Ole Oscar," announced the Swine Master to the cheering crowd. "Next, Glorious Gabby is neck-to-neck with 'Ole Oscar...with Merry Missy followin' right behind. They're making their way around the track, and it's 'Ole Oscar and now, oh, will ya' look at that folks? It's Glorious Gabby coming up from behind," cried out the astonished Swine Master.

Everyone stood and applauded, as Glorious Gabby with her slightly, bowed legs, ran with all of her might, knowing, *'I AM a Winner!'*

The little girl in the pink pants cheered her on, and called out to Glorious Gabby, "You can do it...*You are a Winner*!" And that was the only voice Glorious Gabby could hear. For the first time, Glorious Gabby had crossed the finished line.

"And it's Glorious Gabby—that's our Grand Prize Winner today!" The Swine Master announced to a crowd, who could barely hear him over the enthusiastic cheering.

Friends and families began chanting, "Gab-by, Gab-by, Gab-by," as she panted, still in disbelief. She looked up, only to see the little girl in the pink pants.

"I told you, Gabby, you *are* a winner," called out the girl to her racing star.

"And now, let's get our best, pig cheerer down from the stands."

The little girl in the pink pants approached the *Winner's Circle*, smiling. She, too, had a little limp to her walk, but she made her way down to the gallery, full of people, and with pride, she stood next to Glorious Gabby.

"You are the Grand Prize Winner today, my dear," adorning the little girl with a pig nose over her head.

The crowd cheered, as she smiled with a wide grin. She reached down to give Glorious Gabby a big hug, and to tell her that she indeed, was a winner. Photographers came up to take pictures of the two of them together.

The Swine Master made the big announcement, "And now folks, the Grand Prize Winner not only receives valuable coupons for treats at the Fair, this young lady gets to ride in the *BIG PARADE*, right alongside Glorious Gabby!"

The little girl kissed Glorious Gabby's ear, and looked her straight in her true, ebony eyes and whispered, "See you at the *Parade!*"

As they made their way down the grandstand and back through the busy fairgrounds, off the families raced to stand in line for the *Merry-go-Round*.

On the carousel, the little girl in the pink pants asked her mother if she could climb on the pink pig wearing the golden crown.

Her Mother helped her up, with her slow leg, and she sat on top, as if a princess herself. Round and round, round and round they circled on the carousel, as it played a sweet melody.

As the circles of the carousel slowly stopped, families exited to see the final showstoppers before evening set upon them. There were pony rides, shopping, and more games to be played, and of course, more tasty treats to be enjoyed!

As the day darkened into early night, children and families were ready to sit curbside and enjoy the *FAIR PARADE*. The Swine Master gathered with the town mayor, and placed the little girl with the pink pants on top of the red wagon. Next to her was Glorious Gabby, adorned with her *first place* blue ribbon. Everyone stood to salute our American Flag, held by one of the marching band members. Old Uncle Sam came too, standing tall on stilts as he waved, 'Ole Glory.'

The little girl in the pink pants and Glorious Gabby made their way down Main Street to the tune, "*Stars and Stripes Forever*." Together, they sat proudly, knowing they were both winners, after all.

"I just *knew* that you could do it, Gabby." And with that, she gave Gabby one more kiss on her floppy, brown and pink ear, as the two winners headed down Main Street.

They were enjoying the ride of their lives — side by side, in first place, together.

The End

Deborah Burggraaf was born in Danbury, Connecticut and moved to southern California. She lived there for thirty years, and now resides in Palm Beach County, Florida, teaching middle school for nearly twenty years.

Mrs. Burggraaf embraced her love for writing and began to write stories with messages for children. She takes everyday simple wonders and unfolds them into inspirational outcomes for children.

She continues to motivate young minds each day, inspiring children to believe in themselves and to follow their dreams in life.

AT THE PIG RACES is **Mrs. Burggraaf's** sixth book, which includes: *Caught in the Middle, Cooka, the Bird without Wings, Boonie--Freedom Runner, Crow No More and Hot Wheels for Benny*.

 On her website: **dburgg.com**, you can download activities for each book, as well as contact the author, or schedule an appearance by **Mrs. Burggraaf**:

www.dburgg.com

email: deb@dburgg.com

Phone: 561-429-6733

MATT LUMSDEN is a graphic artist and author based in Boca Raton, Florida. **Mr. Lumsden** enjoys writing, drawing, and hanging out with his best friend, "*Snoop*." **Mr. Lumsden's** books, *Dogs in the Bed* and *Puppy Love*, are available on his website or by contacting him directly at the email shown below:

Matt_lumsden@yahoo.com

android.market.com/apps

Mr. Lumsden's creative mind and design lure the reader into each story, with simplicity at its finest; yet vibrant colors leave the reader breathless, with every turn of the page.